Gus and Buster
work things out

YEARLING BOOKS are designed especially to entertain and enlighten young people. The finest available books for children have been selected under the direction of Charles F. Reasoner, Professor of Elementary Education, New York University.

For a complete listing of all Yearling titles,
write to Education Sales Department, Dell Publishing Co., Inc.,
1 Dag Hammarskjold Plaza, New York, N.Y. 10017

Gus and Buster
work things out

story by Andrew Bronin

illustrated by Cyndy Szekeres

A YEARLING BOOK

Published by
Dell Publishing Co., Inc.
1 Dag Hammarskjold Plaza
New York, New York 10017

Text copyright © 1975 by Andrew Bronin
Illustrations copyright © 1975 by Cyndy Szekeres

Yearling ® TM 913705, Dell Publishing Co., Inc.
ISBN: 0-440-43318-5
Reprinted by arrangement with Coward, McCann & Geoghegan, Inc.
Printed in the United States of America
Sixth Dell Printing—August 1978

CONTENTS

1. THE BUNK BED

"I want
the bottom bunk," said Gus.
"I want the bottom bunk too,"
said Buster.
"We will flip for it," said Gus.
Gus took a shiny coin
from his pocket.
"Heads or tails?" he asked.
"Tails," said Buster.
Gus flipped the coin
high in the air and caught it.
"Heads," said Gus. "You lose."
And he put the coin in his pocket.

"You didn't let me see it,"
said Buster.

"Don't you trust me?" asked Gus.

"If I were in the desert
and you had all the water,
I would trust you," said Buster.

"If I were climbing a mountain
and you were holding the rope,
I would trust you," said Buster.

"But when it comes to bunk beds,"
said Buster, "I do not trust you."

"All right," said Gus.
"I will let you see the coin.
I will flip it and
let it land on the floor.
If it comes up heads, I will win.
If it comes up tails,
you will lose."
"That is fair," said Buster.

Gus flipped the coin.

It landed on the floor.

"Tails," he said. "You lose."

He patted Buster's shoulder.

"You will like the top bunk,"

he said.

Gus lay down in the bottom bunk.

Buster climbed up to the top bunk.

He tucked his sheets in tight.

He fluffed up his pillow.

He moved around

until he was comfortable.

Then he moved around some more.

"Buster!" said Gus.

"Stop moving around!"

"I'm sorry," said Buster.

And he lay very still.

Buster lay still for a long time.
"Gus," he said,
"I can't sleep in the top bunk.
It is too high."
"Try harder," said Gus.

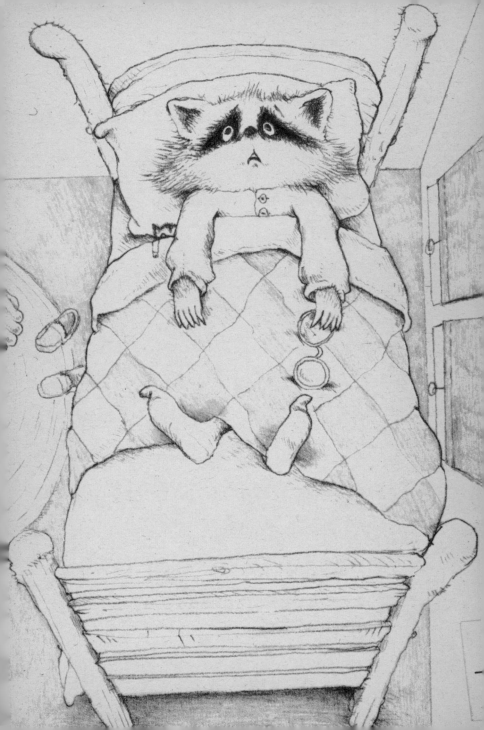

Buster tried counting sheep.

He counted a thousand and three.

He was still awake.

Buster tried to put himself

to sleep bit by bit.

"Go to sleep, toes," he whispered.

His toes fell asleep.

"Go to sleep, feet," he whispered.

His feet fell asleep.

"Go to sleep, legs," he whispered.

His legs fell asleep.

But by the time he got to his knees

his toes were wide awake again.

"Gus?" said Buster.

"Are you awake?"

"How can I sleep when you
are whispering to your toes?"
said Gus.

Gus bit his sheet.

"If I give you the bottom bunk,"
he said, "will you go to sleep?"

"Yes," said Buster. "I promise."

They switched bunks.

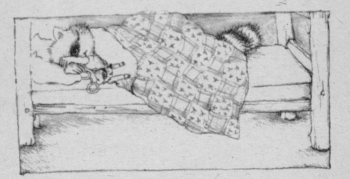

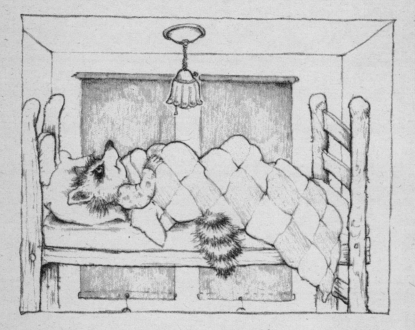

Buster crawled into Gus' warm bed.

"Thank you, Gus," he said.

"I am almost asleep already."

And in a moment, he was.

Gus lay in the top bunk,

and stared at the ceiling.

2. LIVING ROOM DAY

It was Saturday morning.

Tip-a-tap-a-tip went the roof.

Plink, plunk, plink
went the windowpane.

Buster and Gus lay in their beds
and stared out the window.

"It is raining," said Buster.

"It looks like a living room day."

"What is a living room day?"
asked Gus.

"That is a day when it is raining,
and you can't play outside,"
said Buster.

"So you play in the living room."

"Oh," said Gus.

Gus and Buster got out of bed.

Buster washed his face.

He brushed his teeth.

He went over to the toy box

and opened it.

It was empty.

Gus was sitting in the living room.

All the toys were spread

around him on the floor.

"I got here first," said Gus.

"You can have the toys

I don't want."

He gave Buster the baseball glove,

the baseball bat, and the bicycle.

Buster stared at the glove,
the bat, and the bicycle.
"Gus, these are no good
for a living room day.
They are sunny day toys."
"Who knows?" said Gus.
"Maybe it will get sunny."

Gus played with the toy cars.
He played with
the monkey-on-a-ladder.
He played with the building set.
Buster sat on the bicycle
and watched.
Gus looked up and smiled.
"Cheer up, Buster," he said.
"It may get sunny any minute."

Buster turned
and gazed out the window.
"Lots and lots of clouds," he said.
"But farther on, there is sunshine.
And the sunshine is getting closer."

Gus looked out the window.
He saw the sunshine
getting closer, too.

"Buster, I have been very selfish,"
he said. "You can have
the living room day toys.
I will take the outside toys."

"Are you sure?" asked Buster.

"Yes," said Gus.

"I have been very, very selfish."

Buster scratched his head.

He pulled his whiskers.

"No," he said. "I think

I will keep the toys I have."

Soon the sun was out.

Buster put on his baseball mitt.

He swung his bat over his shoulder.

He rode the bicycle off

to the baseball field.

Gus sat on the floor
and wished for rain.

3. TABLE MANNERS

It was breakfast time.

Gus made the orange juice.

Buster made the pancakes.

They sat down at the table

and began to eat.

"Chomp, chomp, chomp,"

went Buster.

"Good, chomp chomp chomp."

Buster opened his mouth wide

on every bite. Gus could see

all the chewed-up pancake inside.

"Yechh, Buster," said Gus.

"Stop that."

"Stop what?" asked Buster.

"Stop chewing
with your mouth open."

"I do not chew with my
mouth open," said Buster.

"Yes, you do," said Gus.

"And you are talking
with your mouth full."

"Only because you
talked to me first," said Buster.

Buster took another bite.
"Chomp chomp chomp," he went.
"Buster!" said Gus.
"You are doing it again!"
Buster opened his eyes
wide in surprise.
"I am not," he said.

Gus left the room.

In a minute he came back.

He had a mirror.

He held it in front of Buster.

Buster watched himself eat.
"I do open my mouth a little,"
he said. "I am sorry. I will stop."

Buster took another
forkful of pancake.
This time he kept his mouth
closed tight.
But he didn't chew.
He just sat there
with his cheeks bulging.

"Why aren't you chewing?"
asked Gus.
"Why are you sitting there
with a mouth full of food?"
"Ummmphh, mmmphhh,"
said Buster.
"Swallow your food and then talk,"
said Gus.
"Ummmmphh, mmmphhh,"
said Buster.
Gus stared at him.

Buster ran to the bedroom
and got a pad and pencil.
He ran back to the kitchen.
He wrote a note.
"Dear Gus," it said,
"I cannot chew
with my mouth closed.
And when I cannot chew,
I cannot swallow.
And when I cannot swallow,
my mouth is full.
And you said I shouldn't talk
when my mouth is full.
Your brother, Buster."

"Open your mouth and chew,"
said Gus.

Buster opened his mouth.

He chewed as fast as he could.

He swallowed and gasped for air.

"I can't chew with my mouth
closed," he said. "It is impossible!"

"No, it isn't," said Gus.

"Look. I can do it."

And he did.

"But I am not you," said Buster.

"How could you be?" asked Gus.

"Look, Buster," Gus said.
"I know what is wrong.
You are not just closing your lips.
You are closing your teeth, too.
Close your lips, but not your teeth."

Buster pressed his lips tight
together. Then he tried to chew.
"Ouch!" he said.
"What happened?" asked Gus
"I bit my cheek!" said Buster.

Gus thought.

"I've got it," he said.

"Press your lips tight together.

Then pull out your cheeks

with your hands. *Then* chew."

Buster pressed his lips together.

He pulled his cheeks out.

He chewed up and down.

It worked.

"There," said Gus.

"Now just do that when you eat!"

Buster cut a piece of pancake.

He put it in his mouth.

He put his knife and fork down.

He pulled his cheeks out
and chewed.

"Good!" said Gus.

"Now do it again!"

Buster did it again.

But as he did, two big tears
rolled down to his whiskers
and hung there.

"Buster!" said Gus.

"Why are you crying?"

"Because eating is no fun anymore,"
said Buster.

"It is too much work."

Gus looked at Buster.
"Buster, I am sorry. Stop crying
and eat any way you want."

Buster dried his eyes
and started to eat again.
Gus tried not to listen.

4. THE TELEVISION SET

Gus got soda from the refrigerator.

He got pretzels from the cupboard.

He put on his football sweat shirt.

He put on his football helmet.

He went into the living room

to watch the football game.

The television was already on.
Buster was watching
a checkers game.

"Buster," said Gus, "you will
have to leave. I am going
to watch a football game."
"I can't leave now," said Buster.
"The checkers game just began."

"I have been waiting
for this football game all week,"
said Gus.
"I bought soda for this game.
I bought pretzels for this game.
I put on my sweat shirt
and helmet for this game.
And I am going to watch it."
He turned the knob
on the television.

"Gus," said Buster.

"Turn that back."

"*Everyone* watches football!"
shouted Gus.

"*No one* watches checkers!"

"I am not everyone," said Buster.

Buster turned
the television knob forward.
Gus turned the knob backward.
The knob came off.
Gus couldn't put it back on.
Neither could Buster.
"Now you've done it," they said
to each other at the same time.

Gus took his soda and pretzels
and sweat shirt and helmet
and sat on the front stoop.

Buster sat
in front of the television and
watched the lines go up and down.

Soon Buster went out to see Gus.

"Gus, would you like
to play football?"

"Yes!" said Gus.

They played
until the sun went down.
Gus won most of the games.
But Buster won the last one.

"Buster," said Gus,

"would you like to play checkers?"

"Yes!" said Buster.

And they played until bedtime.

Buster won most of the games.

But Gus won the last one.

Gus leaned down
from the top bunk.
"Buster," he said,
"Did you let me win the last
checkers game on purpose?"
"Of course not!" said Buster.

"Did you let me win the last football game on purpose?"
"Of course not!" said Gus.

And they both fell asleep smiling.

About the Author

ANDREW BRONIN grew up on Long Island and was graduated from Columbia College in New York. He has written books for children on sports, history, and science, including two *What Lives There* books for Coward, McCann & Geoghegan, *The Desert* and *The Cave*. Andrew Bronin is currently completing his studies for an MD at New York Medical College and plans to pursue a dual career of practicing medicine and writing.

About the Artist

"It's more fun to draw brotherly squabbles than it is to listen to them," comments CYNDY SZEKERES, who adds, "The vivid memories of verbal conflicts between my own two sons inspired the illustrations for this book."

Cyndy Szkeres, her husband, fine artist Gennaro Prozzo, and their sons, Marc and Chris, have recently moved to the country from Brooklyn, New York, and are enjoying the change of pace and scene in Putney, Vermont. A graduate of Pratt Institute, the artist has given pleasure to many children with her acclaimed illustrations for *Four-Ring Three, Pippa Mouse, Little Richard,* and *Moon Mouse*—to mention but four of her delightful creations.